CASY LACY:
WAS ONCE A
BULLY
NOW
SHE IS OUR
FRIEND

Look with your eyes, and you will see sitting amongst all these beautiful trees, is Vladimir's Vizard Academy (V.V.A.). It's a quirky school and sometimes a bit spooky, but the V.V.A. is a place where Sumpkinville children come to learn, play, and make friends each school day.

Mr. Vladimir is the principal at the V.V.A., and he wants his school to be perfect in every way, so he created this school policy:

- Find A Friend
- Keep A Friend
- Learn together

Today is a special day at the V.V.A... because it's Casy Lacy's first day. Casy and her family just moved to Sumpkinville all the way from Smillington, U.S.A.

Coach Doglum introduces her to everyone in gym class. "Good Morning everyone, this is Casy Lacy, she comes to us from Smillington, and she loves karate."

It's Batball day. Batball is a competitive game in which children use Dashroids to knock down the bats that are hanging from the ceiling. Coach Doglum calls this a sport, but most parents consider it pest control. The team that knocks down the most bats, wins!

As you can see, Casy is very sad; it looks like she wasn't picked for a team.

Do you think that this is the way she thought her first day of school would be?

Here is Professor Dolan's classroom, but all the kids call him Professor D; he teachers Breedology 101, which is the art of mixing two animals into one. When the process is complete, a monkey can have duck feet!

Late again, it's the same every day; Professor D. rushes into the class, 'Sorry, guys, I forgot we had a class, let's see what's on the agenda today. Is it a unicorn and a phoenix?"

The whole class shouts out NO!

"Oh, wait, you are right. We are on chicken and foxes. Herbert, can you tell me what you get when you combine these two animals?"

Now, everyone at the V.V.A. knows that when Herbert gets nervous, he hiccups a lot, so when Professor D. called on Herbert, he froze. Instantly, the hiccups started coming and wouldn't stop! Poor Herbert stood at the front of the class frozen in fear, hiccuping so loud that everyone in the class could hear.

Casy Lacy laughed loudly at Herbert then stood up and said, "Everyone knows that answer! It's a chickenpox."

Herbert's friends were not impressed. Casy is not acting very nice; surely, she won't make any new friends acting this way.

Mrs. Myth has the grooviest classroom at the V.V.A. In this class, students learn about peace, love, and grooviness. Of course, today's lesson is about peace. Mrs. Myth begins class by asking, "Students, can you tell me what this symbol is?"

Without raising her hand, Casy blurts out and says," I know what it is because I know everything, and I am way smarter than all of you."

All the other students seem to be annoyed, and wonder, why Casy is acting this way. Do you think you know why she is acting this way?

The playground is a child's favorite place; it is there where they get to run, play, and have fun with their friends each day.

Sadly, Casy is not having fun today. Herbert and his friends were very annoyed at the way she behaved, so they decided not to invite her to play.

THINK ABOUT IT

Later that day, Mr. Vladimir called Casy into the Think About it Room.
This is the room where children go, to think about their choices.
Mr. Vladimir welcomes her by saying,
"Good afternoon, Casy, so how is your first day at the V.V.A.?

"Terrible in a very awful way!"

"In the gym, they wouldn't let me play Batball, and during recess,
no one even talked to me!""No one wants to be my friend,
or let me play with them!"

Mr. Vladimir asks in a very caring way,
"Casy, have you been nice to everyone all day?"

"Well, no! But that is because they made me mad and sad!"

Mr. Vladimir very wisely said, "Well, Casy, not letting you play Batball I think was a
mistake, but even good people make mistakes, and two wrongs never make a right.
Do you think it's possible that making fun of Herbert, and acting like you knew
everything made it where no one wanted to play with you?
"Maybe!" Said Casy.

Then Mr. Vladimir asked, "I bet if you could give them a second chance that
they would give you one as well. Do you think you could do that?"

Shortly after Casy left, Simon and his friends are called into the
Think About it Room.

Once they are all settled in, Mr. Vladimir says to them,
"I was a bit disappointed today when I saw Casy sitting alone at recess.
Can you tell me why?"

Herbert tries to answer, but cannot stop hiccuping, so Simon answers for him.
"Mr. Vladimir, Casy is a BIG BULLY!"

Mr. Vladimir sighs and says, "I am not saying that what Casy did was right,
but it's not always easy being the new kid and I think what happened today
is like Breedology in many ways. We combined two wrongs and created Bullies."

"Bullies???" Asked Alice and went on to say, "Casy is the only bully."

Mr. Vladimir replies, "Children, today is Casy's first day, and instead of being
invited to play, she was left alone to watch everyone else play.
I think if you tried to include her, she might stop being a bully.
Why don't you try this and see what happens?"

THINK ABOUT IT

So, the next day, everyone was kind all day. Casy got to play Batball, and because she is so tall, she helped the team win.

Simon, Herbert, and their other friends decided to invite Casy to play on the playground. They all made a new friend.

FIND A FRIEND

KEEP A FRIEND

LEARN TOGETHER

It's not always easy for people to make friends, but so often, misunderstandings and simple mistakes cause hurtful feelings that prevent friendships. If we are all kind to one another and try to include everyone in our groups, then the V.V.A. and other schools will always be a place for children to learn, play, and make friends each school day.

Contributing Authors

Landri Mueller

Kasia Richardson

Landri Mueller is 9 years old and dreams of being an architect when she grows up. Landri is a kindhearted, outgoing, friendly child. She loves everything art and in her spare time you will catch her at her desk drawing. Her hobbies include volleyball, arts & crafts, karate, and swimming.

Kasia Richardson is 10 years old and aspires to be a photographer when she grows up. Kasia is very loving and kind hearted. She has a love for her art. She enjoys playing volleyball, spending time with her friends and loves her family and Jesus.

LAVERNIA INTERMEDIATE

CONTRIBUTING AUTHORS

JENNA TALBERT

Jenna Talbert is a sweet, energetic 9 year old that loves cheerleading and running track. She enjoys spending time with her friends, family, being at church and doing crafts. She has dreams of being a teacher or financial advisor when she grows up.

KALYNN GOODE

Kalynn Goode is 10 years old and wants to be a news reporter or fashion designer when she grows up. Kalynn is not afraid of the spotlight. As she enjoys acting, singing, dancing and playing the piano and guitar.

LAVERNIA INTERMEDIATE

CONTRIBUTING AUTHORS

CLAYTON GRELLE

Clayton Grelle is 10 years old who aspires to be a chef. He loves to read, make others laugh, swim, sing and dance. Clayton is eager to learn, he is kind hearted, and outgoing.

AUDREY LAPACKA

Audrey Lapacka is an exceptional 10 year old who enjoys playing soft ball and reading. She has a passion for travel and helping others. Audrey hopes to one day be a famous artist or author.

Lavernia Intermediate
Contributing Authors

Brooke Dever

Brooke Emma Dever is 10 years old and wants to be a baker when she grows up. She is a fun loving imaginative person who loves animals. Brooke enjoys baking with her Mimi and   gardening with her Papa. She loves new adventures and spending time with her family.

Avery Keck

Avery Keck is a 10 year old, kind hearted 4th grader. She dreams of being in marketing when she grows up. In her spare time she enjoys playing volleyball andspending time with her friends and family. She is an amazing daughter and little sister!
Her strong faith in God inspires us. We know she will accomplish many great things.

Keagan Gulley

Keagan Shea Gulley is 10 years old and she aspires to be a Chef when she grows up. Keagan is a spunky, fun-loving child who loves helping others. She enjoys cheer, tumbling, and playing soccer with her two sisters. She also has a great love of history.

FAN PAGES

SUMPKINVILLE CHARACTERS
FROM LAVERNIA INTERMEDIATE

Cayleigh Cervanka is 10 years old. Cayleigh enjoys tumbling and cheer. At home, Cayleigh can be found in the pool. On the trampoline, or feeding all the animals on our farm. She is loving, sweet, and caring young lady. When Cayleigh grows up she wants to be a nurse.

CAYLEIGH CERVANKA

Madelynn F. Nagelmueller is 8 years old and wants to be a singer when she grows up. She loves playing volleyball and building with Legos. She has a huge heart, is adventurous and loves making new friends.

MADELYNN NAGELMUELLER

Zoey Wood is 11 years old. She is a yellow belt in Karate and plays the saxophone. She loves swimming, singing and dancing. She is very sweet and cares for others feelings.

ZOEY WOOD

Logan Johnson is 10 years old. He would like to be a software engineer when he gets older. He loves to play video games, and read books, swim and tease his sister. He loves math and science. Logan is a really nice kid.

LOGAN JOHNSON

Bryar Crane is a 9 year old in the 4th grade. He enjoys playing soccer and listening to music. Bryar loves to spend time with his older brother Bryce. He wants to one day be a Navy Seal. Bryar loves to lend a hand to help out his teacher.

BRYAR CRANE

SUMPKINVILLE CHARACTERS

JORDON FINCH

LANDON DENTON

Jordan D. Finch is 9 years old and wants to be in the entertainment industry. She loves dressing up, acting, singing, dancing and drawing. She is a loving, sweet and caring young lady who loves being a social butterfly.

Landon Denton is 7 years old. Landon wants to be the United States President when he grows up. He loves to read, play Minecraft, and play outside on his family farm. Landon is a sweet, silly, smart kid who likes to wear green.

SUMPKINVILLE CHARACTERS

NATHAN HOUSLEY

Nathan Housley is 6 years old and wants to be a teacher when he grows up. He enjoys Legos and playing baseball. He is excited to be in this book with his best friend Zoe. He can't wait to share this book with his family and friends.

EANNA DUNN

Eanna B. Dunn is 8 years old and wants to be a veterinarian when she grows ups. She is very adventurous but also loves to curl up with a good book.

SUMPKINVILLE CHARACTERS

Cash S. Flippen is 6 years old and in 1st grade. He enjoys building with Legos and playing Minecraft. Cash is very helpful to others and is always caring towards his friends.

CASH FLIPPEN

Michael Elroy is 11 years old. He plays the piano and trombone and has acted on stage. He enjoys making videos for his YouTube channel and wants to open a technology-aimed business when he grows up. Hot chips and Mexican candy are two of his favorite things.

MICHAEL McELROY

Keane Michael Rhodes is 6 years old and loves playing football. Keane likes dinosaurs and wants to be an archeologists when he grows up. At home, Keane likes to read and play with his three dogs.

KEANE RHODES

SUMPKINVILLE CHARACTERS

Zoe Grace Menchey is 6 years old and has aspirations of being a swimmer when she grows up. Zoe is an inquisitive, loving and outgoing little girl who loves to read, and play soccer and board games.

Cyler M. Tietgens is 9 years old and wants to be a Navy SEAL. He loves playing baseball with his friends. Cyler has a huge heart and is always willing to lend a helping hand.

Reece William Kieffer is 7 years old and would like to be a doctor when he grows up. He loves to swim, dance, and go the beach. He is very smart, loving boy with a wild imagination who truly enjoys life.

ZOE MENCHEY

CYLER TIETGENS

REECE KIEFFER

www.csbinnovations.com

CPSIA information can be obtained at www.ICGtesting.com
Printed in the USA
BVIW12n0834171018
530328BV00007B/4